unheard soliloquies

An Anthology Curated by

Srija Sanyal

Inkfeathers Publishing
www.inkfeathers.com

Unheard Soliloquies
Edited & Compiled by Srija Sanyal
Print Edition

First Published in India in 2022
Inkfeathers Publishing
New Delhi 110095

ISBN 9789390882212

www.inkfeathers.com

Featuring the writings of

Abhishek Agarwal, Bornali Nath Dowerah

Ginni Malik, Hrishikesh Mokashi, Maxine Mathew

Neeraja Krishnaswami, Vaishnavi Tawade

Hiya Banerjee, Srija Sanyal, Anurag Pandey

Aksheeta Chandok (Ash), Kriti Garg

Disclaimer

The anthology 'Unheard Soliloquies' is a collection of 12 short stories and 9 poems written by 12 authors who belong to different parts of the world.

Unless otherwise indicated, all the names, characters, objects, businesses, places, events, incidents- whether physical/non-physical, real/unreal, tangible/ intangible in whatsoever description used in this book are either the product of the author's imagination or used in a fictitious manner. Any resemblance to actual persons, objects, entities, living or dead, or actual events is purely coincidental.

The poems & stories published in this book are solely owned by their respective authors and are in no way intended to hurt anyone's religious, political, spiritual, brand, personal or fanatic beliefs and/or faith, whatsoever. In case, any sort of plagiarism is detected in the contents within this anthology or in case of any complaints, grievances, or objections, neither the anthology editor nor the publisher is to be held responsible.

Contents

Poems

About the Editor

Srija Sanyal

Srija Sanyal is an academic researcher and a Kolkata-born Delhi-ite bibliophile and currently heads the content team at a market research firm. She metamorphoses to a couch-potato cosying up with a nice cup of coffee or a glass of wine, watching episodes of Suits or Boston Legal when not working. Good food and sleep are the two most important things to her in the world. She firmly believes that a panda is her spirit animal, and she can live on biryani and burgers for the rest of her life. An aspiring novelist and an avid reader, she loves to scroll through classical literature, and occasionally pens her thoughts down on paper while binging on Netflix shows.

Editor's Note

The ability to feel—this is something that not everyone possesses. Compassion and empathy are some of those rare elements that are either there in you by default or are just not there at all. And yet, each one of us is surprised in many moments wherein something or someone simply moves us, forcing us to unlearn and shed off the didactic dialogues. This anthology chronicles such moments of epiphany where "feelings" overwhelm the soul and the mind, thus inevitably leading to countless words running through our minds at an unfathomable speed, ready to burst out through the lips or the pen's nip or through any other outlet that it can find. Showcasing some of such moments of epiphanies through short stories and poems, and diary entries, this anthology brings forth the sensibilities of the senses that we often experience but rarely speak about.

Acknowledgements

I have to start by thanking my awesome mother, Chinmoyee Sanyal. From discussing with me enthusiastically the ideas to taking care of everything else while I work on this, she was as important to this anthology journey as I was. Thank you so much, my Polar Bear mommy. The other most important person to thank is Uma Bokil, Publishing Manager, Inkfeathers Publishing, for being a crucial guiding force regarding the technicalities of how to go about things whenever I felt clueless in deciding the next step.

And lastly, thank you to all of the amazing contributors who trusted me with their stories and works of creativity and were patiently considerate throughout this process, which has been a prolonged one for diversified reasons.

Thank you so much, guys!

With Love,

Srija Sanyal

Short
Stories

The Binary Mind

Abhishek Agarwal

I: Sshhh… I am on a mission. A secret mission! A mission which has to be concealed from others.

Mike: Why?

There was a time when Thomas Anthony, Head of the militant, had enquired about the same, and today, he is the CEO of a multinational company in Scotland. Whatever happened completely transformed his being, I recalled, while paraphrasing the same to Mike.

It was twilight, the streets were getting vacant and people rushing to their respective habitats. The local police alarmed the people about the ongoing predicament in the city. The militant troops who wanted to overrule the government created commotion in the streets. Thomas Anthony was leading the troop. Their only aim being to rule the state and were adamant on not going into any kind of negotiation with the present government. They were a team of passionate minds brimming with the fervour of acquiring power in its absolute sense.

Sam Woz, the Chief of the police force sent a message through one of his messengers to Thomas Anthony citing the wrong deeds he and his troops were into, the repercussions of which would be catastrophic if not ceased immediately and asked to meet for a settlement. But what stood out in the message to Thomas is the repeated asking of the reason… the why… that Sam Woz insisted upon. Why did he want to do so? What was his war with the state locals? These questions kept on echoing in Thomas's mind as he quested his second command, Mac Rogers, for an answer.

Mac Rogers: My Honourable Chief, we are a follower of our leader, who matches our passion. You are our leader. We only follow your commands. We owe unquestionable obedience to your words.

Such a rigid framework for an answer hitched Thomas Anthony further, the words hitting him harder more than ever, as if reasserting the echo of the Why thrown at Thomas mercilessly by Sam Woz.

Holding his glass of wine Thomas Anthony sat aloof. He gazed at his fiercely loyal team, the followers vibrant with obedience and devotion. He asked them to leave him in solitude for the moment pondering over the question asked by the police chief. Sipping his wine, he experienced a quiet moment with himself in an attempt to listen to his inner instincts. Something from deep within was eager to come out, which seemed always unattended, he lately realised.

He learned in that particular moment that there were several things rooted deep within his mind which always went unheard; although he heard it daily but let it pass…

unnoticed, unheard. He always opinionated that what he wanted he was already practicing and did not find it necessary to sit in solitude to hear out the speech his mind had to say. Now, in this very moment, he asked himself: why was he actually doing things? Why was he a militant? Why had he wanted to rule the state?

Slowly and steadily, various things kept ushering in into his thoughts. The past days, moments, experiences, all were now coming back. Previously, he worked at a roadside café. Every day was similar to each other with humdrums. Addressing people's unruly demands, spending each day with the servitude that had an unruly connotation attached, Thomas remembered now that he actually got irritated with what he was doing. And there was enough reason for that; the peanut salary after day-long hard work could not even meet the basic needs of his daily life. The skeleton of a failure system of the state exposed itself shamelessly through citizens like Thomas who inhabited the lowest pedestal of the social hierarchy. Thomas, today, sitting in solitude, recalled each of the moments, of those experiences, which propelled his being toward the life of a militant leader challenging the democratic methodology. He now realised that what he really sought was a life of significance and anything less appealed as nothing but pedestrian to him.

He could connect the dots now. His intense urge to lead a life of significance—a meaningful life, failing to achieve which he channelised himself to become a militant and spread terror. He did give a meaning to his life, but he achieved it by spreading fear. He had now achieved the importance and recognition he always has wanted but it was derived out of spreading terror and fear amongst the common people. Now, as his wine glass was empty, he refilled it and sat down again, pondering, was that the only way to fulfil his desires? His mind gave him flashbacks of Nelson Mandela, Mahatma Gandhi, Barack Obama, Sir Ratan Tata, Sir Richard Branson who had gained great popularity, recognition, and great position in their lives by their true selves and by routing through the road of love without any sort of nuisance or terrors caused, ever. In his moment of epiphany, he realised from within that if these personalities could attain such an honourable position in their lives by sheer dedication of following the path of love, why couldn't he? He, too, had the choice to route himself toward this path, but he chose the other path; a path less travelled but also the path of spreading terror and fear.

For a moment, Thomas felt a sharp pain emerging from within himself—the pain of guilt. The epiphanous moment of choosing the wrong path was more than ever at this very moment to him. He further realised that all these days he did not have any war with anyone, be it be the government, the people in general or any other living entities. The war was always with his own self.

The soliloquy of his mind, which was always unheard by his own self, thus far, was finally felt heard as Thomas was gearing to undo his deeds. That very moment, he realised the importance of self-talk and the relation of one with one's own self. This feeling gave him a zest to be what he always wanted to be; but this time, it would be in a noble and a rather virtuous way. He even realised that deep within, he never wanted to spread terror or any sort of chaos anywhere; it was only because he became outrageous and stern with himself, avoiding his internal communication and not hearing out what was going within, that landed him into being an epitome of terror and fear. Lately, now as he heard his internal dialogues and monologues which always kept popping up internally but left unattended to, he understood what he was supposed to do now. He immediately called up his troop and cajoled them to refrain from any terrific acts henceforth and asked to stop all the commotions they have created everywhere.

Deep within he also realised that since all these troops were his followers and merely followed his commands, he should be an example to all of them by being a true leader who set up a path of righteousness. This realisation gave him more impetus to spread love. This was indeed an epiphanous moment for Thomas Anthony, a passionate and action-oriented personality, who surrendered to the police at the end of that day. His transformation was not unnoticed by Sam Woz, who appreciated the metamorphosis that Thomas underwent in solitude and emerged finally as a phoenix to the virtuous path.

Mike: Wow! I can't believe how a brutal militant force like Thomas Anthony and his troops, within a matter of a moment, underwent such a significant transformation and are living a peaceful and respectful life now. It is indeed quite inspiring. But what was the mission you were talking about in the very beginning and why it has to be concealed from others?

I: You really want to know my secret mission? I guessed you forgot about it.

Mike: Quite eager to know!

I: In today's world, we all have one thing in common: lack of time. We are so much entangled with our chores that we tend to ignore important stuff. We have time for others and the outer world, but when it comes for our own self, we tend to let go of it and get twirled with the outside activities. Our mind has many things to share with us, it knows where it wants to go, how it wants to be treated, and what would be the right option for us; all of which are primitive but immensely significant for us to know. But twisted in the worldly affairs, we tend to bypass our internal communication and all our internal talks are left unattended and unheard. Let me ask you this question, Mike; if we don't hear to our own selves, then who will?

Mike responded by nodding, signifying his agreement to me.

While I and Mike went on to ponder further on various other things, my mind was brimming with innumerable epiphanies and soliloquies that I often come face to face with. The mind, sitting quietly within our brain, offers so much most of which we tend to avoid. It has a lot to share with us, but we don't give the importance to hear it out. Hence, we land up doing unworthy, rogue things which aren't for us, like in the case of Thomas Anthony who went about a completely untoward way. But as he had an internal communication and hearing out of what his mind has to say, he retrieved his steps back toward his true calling.

I: The secret mission I was talking about was my internal communication with my own self, to discover, explore, and realise what I was up to in my life, to know my life's purpose and decide how I should carry on my life further. And such self-talks are always private and shouldn't be applauded by the outer world. This conversation is with our inner world which will further form our nature for the outer world. As Thomas Anthony, lately though, had a deep conversation with his inner self and heard out his emotions, feelings, and all that his mind had to convey, it is then only that formed the decided moment of his life as he took a step forward to transform his life and today as we speak, he is living an honourable life as an CEO of a multinational company.

Mike: I agree. So, does our mind only give answers when we have certain questions unanswered?

I: Not actually. Our mind keeps on sharing with us something or the other. There's something which keeps on going in our mind, continuously. It's up to us when we can sit alone, have a self-talk, hear out the emotions and feelings, it has to share, and gradually, we will realise what and why was it conveying, which eventually leads to our eureka moment. As John Milton once said, '*The mind is its own place and in itself can make a heaven of hell or a hell of heaven.*' It is important to remember, my friend, that everything is there in our mind; we just need to hear it out and we will get the answers to our questions. These soliloquies that we often have with ourselves actually enable us to make fair decisions for ourselves and for others, too!

The Hotel Room at Kaziranga

Bornali Nath Dowerah

'What's wrong with you, Zuby? Publishers are eating me up. Please do something, *yaar*!' Sunita was yelling at me.

I couldn't react. Perhaps, I was withdrawn after losing my parents in the pandemic last year. The guilt of never making it to their last rites haunted me. They left me this big mansion in Dibrugarh town. I have none by me except Benu Da, our old caretaker. The mighty Brahmaputra flowing reminded me of the slipping time whenever I gazed from my terrace facing the river. Benu Da entered with a tray full of fruits, cereals, and sweet lime juice, 'Zuu, have something dear child. You don't eat anything. Why are you punishing yourself? It's not your fault at all.'

With teary eyes I replied, 'Please take these away, Benu Da. I don't feel like eating anything. Kindly leave me alone.' Sunita arrived after few minutes. She was the only friend I had in my hometown. We grew up together in the tea city of Assam, our Dibrugarh. Surrounded by lush, green tea gardens we had fun time with nature. After high school, I left for my studies at Assam Valley School in Tezpur. And from there to Jawaharlal Nehru University and further to Leeds. By that time, I became fully independent. I was working as the Adjunct Lecturer in History after completing my research work in Historical Museums in England from University of Leeds.

During autumn break, I managed to visit my parents in Dibrugarh amidst the pandemic before India was placed in the red list countries. This return shattered my entire life. I'm the only child to my parents—Raghu Baruah and Nimi Baruah. A small and happy family. I could recollect my video conversations with them. '*Maa* and *Paa*, this time, no excuse. You have to come to the U.K. with me. You have lived enough in Dibrugarh. As I get my PR, I'll buy a home here.'

'First you come, Zuu. Who knows if we shall be alive to accompany you?'

'What, *Maa*! Why do you threaten me this way? I'll complain to *Paa*, okay?'

'Just kidding, Zuu. We miss you and so, we always include you in our conversations. Wait, *Paa* is here. He wants to talk.'

'My little princess, how are you? And what's cooking between mother and daughter?'

'Paa…'

Sunita interrupts, 'What are you so engrossed into, Zuby?'

'Sunita…' I couldn't speak further.

'What have you made of yourself, babes?'

She asked Benu Da to leave the tray there and let me eat my breakfast.

'Tell me, Sunita.'

'What to tell you? I want to give you something.'

'What?'

'Here are your booking details and reservation. They gave me a while ago to hand it over to you.' Sunita gave me the papers and details paid by my publishers. That was part of my contract with Ranganadi Publishers. They hired me to write a fiction on Kaziranga. I was supposed to leave earlier, but I couldn't. Now, the next day, I had booking for one week stay at the Green Grass Resort located amidst the dense forest of wildlife and migratory birds.

Sunita and Benu Da encouraged me to do my task. I packed my backpack and my MacBook Air. A Scorpio was waiting for me with a driver. Benu Da packed some food and fruits along with water bottles. Sunita was there with a smile in her face. She hugged me and said, 'I know you'll accomplish the task. All the best. Take care and call me up. I'll poke you in your dinner, lunch, and breakfast hours.'

She handed me a transparent box of medicines and pills for emergency care. She's a physician after all and my support forever. At 7 AM we started off our journey from South Amolapatty area of Dibrugarh. Thanks to Sunita, I carried my RT-PCR negative test reports and double-dose vaccine certificates as well. It took nearly two hours and half to reach Jorhat as the road was free. After crossing Jorhat, I asked the driver to stop for a while. I took out my phone and start clicking photos of the small children who were lost in their fun and diving in a freshwater pond. They must be around eleven or twelve. Their laughter cheered my mood. One of them saw me clicking photos. They waved their little hands at me saying, 'Baido, bye-bye.' I waved them back and went into the car. I returned to them with some packets of chocolates and left the place.

During the journey, I realised where to find happiness. We stopped at Golaghat to have lunch at a roadside Dhaba. I paid the driver to have a non-veg meal, whereas I satiated myself with whatever Benu Da packed for me. After lunch, we continued the journey. Due to the unevenness of roads, we reached the hotel by late afternoon. The driver was put into the dormitory, and I was allotted a suite—number 666.

As I reached my room, I called up both Benu Da and Sunita. My publishing agent called me up to enquire if the room was good enough for me to create a writing ambience. It was a corner suite—far from the boisterous world and the other rooms too. There was a balcony with off-white wooden furniture and a glass table in wooden frame. In front of the balcony there seemed to be a pond surrounded by deodar trees. The helper left my luggage there with a welcoming gesture and asked me about my evening snacks and dinner. I said, 'I'll order on phone. You may go. Take these. Thank you.' I handed him a fifty rupees' note as a tip and relieved him.

The room was quite spacious. A big queen size bed. There was a living room with all wooden furniture. The bathroom had an oval bathtub with sweet-scented soap bars, shampoos, aromatic body oil, toothbrush, and paste. A hairdryer was also there. I took a warm bath. I ordered a plate of pasta and some green coffee.

Till the order arrived, I opened my laptop and was trying to write something about my journey. Winter had not arrived yet, and suddenly, I began to feel a surge of chilling cold through my body. The fan and A.C. were off, yet I was feeling cold. Strangely, there was no breeze that I could experience. I doubled my clothes and popped a fever pill. While I was about to write I felt as if I was being watched. I was unable to concentrate. I checked every nook and corner if there were any hidden cameras. I couldn't locate any. My snacks arrived and I ordered a light dinner—a bowl of chicken soup with mixed veggies.

I opened my laptop to write about the plot and then I'd work upon the characters. Unable to focus on my work I walked towards the balcony that faced the deserted pond. I could hear some sounds as if someone was throwing pebbles into the pond. I imagined my protagonist doing that seated alone by the side. To the left there was a huge mango tree. I didn't notice that a while ago as I just gave a quick look around. In a full moon night while gazing at the tree I noticed a shadowy figure of a girl comfortably sat in one of the branches, moving her legs forward and backward, playfully. Her one handheld a branch and the other hand rested on the branch she was seated. She seemed to be staring at me. I couldn't make out much except her dark long hair and perhaps, a frock that she might me wearing. I shouted, 'Hey, who are you? What are you doing here? You'll fall down.'

There was no response. I could hear her giggles. This made me more anxious. Immediately I entered inside my room. I picked up my phone—there was no tower signals at all. I wondered what I had seen. I called up room service through the hotel phone. Damn! It was not working. What else do I have? I decided to pack my bags and leave the hotel.

God!!! I'm unable to open the door! Am I locked inside? What's happening to me? What's happening around? I was screaming for help—knocking at the door, 'Someone help me! Please! I'm locked inside. Please get me out of here! Please someone… Please!'

Even if I left this hotel where would I go during the night? I was amidst a dense forest in Kaziranga. I tried to sleep but I couldn't—the resonances of pebbles thrown into water, giggles of the mysterious girl and the sight of her shadow looking at me generated uncanny vibes inside me. She didn't harm me physically. The fear was within me—my own creation. I nourished my fear to the extent that it panicked me.

There was only one way to get out of my fear—to complete my task at this room itself. I began war against my fear and sat to write my plot. Just then a thought crossed my mind—searching for any recent past incidents that happened at Green Grass Resort. And to my surprise, there was one dreadful accident last year on 24 March 2020, of a seven-year-old girl who got drowned while playing while her parents were at this resort. Her name was Arhi. When I saw her picture, she resembled the shadowy figure that I encountered to a huge extent.

I found a purpose to execute my plot and protagonist. I closed my eyes and prayed to the innocent soul who left early, to bless me write about her as part of my fiction. I continued writing till the rays of sun reached me through the off-white curtains. Just then the room service knocked. I responded, 'I think I'm locked inside.'

'Ma'am, you've interlocked it from inside. Please turn the knob three times.'

I did as I was directed, and there I stood behind opened door letting my new life enter. Most often we lock ourselves within, despite having the keys with us. Yet, there are certain times when we fail to distinguish the real from the unreal. I did feel a presence inside the room. If it were Arhi ... I don't know. Or perhaps, creation of my memory and imagination.

Serendipity

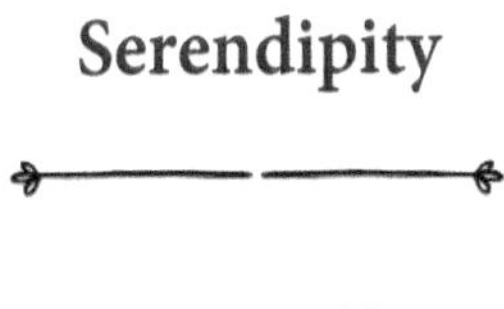

Ginni Malik

I fell short of words. I didn't know how to respond. I just held the juice glass as tightly as I could, trying to refrain from reacting.

These were the friends with whom I had spent so many years of my life. They knew me since childhood. And yet, they were so cruel and reckless with their words. Ceaseless thoughts started crowding my mind as the rolls of laughter continued around me.

'So, Aashi! Tell us something about that Energy Healing stuff you always talk about. Does it even help?' Kriti winked her eye and sipped her soft drink.

'Oh, it's rubbish! All kinds of money-making gimmicks!' Sonal replied while waiting for the *henna* to dry. 'I don't know what made you leave your high-paying job in the UK and come back to India. You are just wasting your time now!'

I had so much to talk about these spiritual practices that

have healed me. I could spend the entire night explaining these concepts and how they calmed me and helped me to let go of the unnecessary control that often sucks away the joy of the present moment. But I chose not to share any of my knowledge and learnings as I knew that the people standing across me had closed themselves off to anything unconventional.

Exhausted of the unending conversations surrounding me, I placed my half-drank juice glass on the nearest table and left the spot. I went outside in search of some fresh air to save myself from the claustrophobic environment inside the bride's room.

I came out of the building and walked towards the lawn. I felt a lump in my throat and was unable to walk further. I halted and sat on the bench that was right beside me.

'These people…these hardened souls claim to be my closest and dearest friends! It's so sad that they are so full of negativity, judgments, and…' I was lost in my thoughts when I heard a harsh voice followed by a crying sound.

I looked around to find the source of the sounds. I spotted a couple standing behind one of the pillars of the main wedding hall. I squinted my eyes but was unable to see anything. I took in a deep breath, got up from the bench, and started walking slowly towards the pillar. Suddenly, I heard the sound of someone sobbing. I turned my head and saw a woman standing behind the tree. I ran up to her and offered help.

'Look, I know that we're strangers to each other, but I saw you crying, so I just came here to check if you are okay.'

The girl looked straight into my eyes and asked, 'Who are you?'

'Hi! I'm Aashi!' I extended my hand.

Surprised at a stranger being so friendly with her, the girl hesitated to introduce herself.

'Oh hello! My name... my name is Neha.'

We shook hands for the very first time.

'Why are you crying?' I asked her.

'I lost my job today!'

'It must be hard, but you'd get a better job,' I replied.

'I don't think I am talented enough.'

'Your worth is not decided by the external factors.'

Neha lowered her head. 'I fail to meet the expectations of people around me. What would you have done if you were at my place?'

I smiled. 'I would have released all control. Once we allow life to happen naturally to us, we can attract everything we want.'

Neha was in complete awe of me. 'How can we remain so strong and calm amidst such a hurricane?' she asked.

I felt heard. I felt as if my words have some value to someone. Instead of discarding everything I had said, she showed curiosity.

I smiled. 'Why don't you learn Energy Healing with me?'

And that was the beginning of our beautiful friendship. The friendship that I started sharing with Neha felt like a breath of fresh air. She was as bright as the ray of hope after a heavy monsoon shower.

She was so inspired by the very concept of spirituality that she expressed interest to know more about the topic and explore the world of Energy Healing in a much better way.

'I could finally work on a personal project that was stuck for the past 6 months!' said Neha one day. 'Thank you so much, Aashi. You helped me heal all the blockages I had.'

I smiled. 'Neha, I have done nothing. You've always had this power.'

I had never imagined that I would bond so well with a stranger. But that's how life is! It sends some special people your way to uplift your spirits and help you become a better version of yourself. That's how Neha and I contributed to each other's life. Even though she was ten years older than me, but that age difference never hampered our friendship.

I started feeling valued and honoured whenever I spent time with Neha. She allowed me to be myself and helped me to become even a better version of myself. Instead of pointing out the bad in me, she unearthed the good in me.

'You are magical, Aashi,' she said to me on the call one night. 'You have so much inside you. I think you should start giving your sessions.'

'Do you think that'd work?' I asked.

'Of course!' Neha replied. 'The world needs to hear your words. Don't keep it all locked inside.'

I started to become more confident and become more aware of my hidden potential. And so, slowly, I started to put myself out there.

'Is it good?' I asked Neha, as I show her one of my Energy Healing posts on Instagram. 'Do you think that people would come to attend the session on Sunday?'

'Of course, Aashi!' Neha replied. 'You only said that once we are in a calm state of mind, we attract everything.'

I took in a deep breath. 'Thanks for the reminder, Neha. I will not worry about it at all.'

And so, it happened. I got 5 people to attend my very first healing session. Throughout my life, I had been made to feel like a loser for leaving my job and choosing an unconventional path. I was forced to fit into a mould, and if I refused to do that, I was criticised. But now, I could finally see my vision manifesting. And Neha was one of the reasons. I had finally tasted the feeling of pure friendship. But something was waiting for us.

Since both of us loved painting, we decided to visit an art museum and attend an exhibition. While we were completely mesmerised by the painter's imagination, I heard a familiar voice calling me from behind.

As I turned my head to face the speaker, my heart sank as I saw Kriti standing in front of me. The long-forgotten humiliating experience during Sonal's wedding suddenly became alive in my memory like a fresh wound.

'Hey, Aashi. What's up?' Kriti asked in her usual boisterous tone.

'I'm fine. What about you?' I asked, trying to be as open towards her as possible.

'I'm great. Getting married in a few months!' Kriti said.

'Oh, congratulations!' I replied excitedly, though I feared

that the conversation might now shift to me not having a date and deciding to remain single all my life.

Throwing a glance at Neha, Kriti spoke again. 'So, when did you start developing an interest in painting? What happened to that Energy thing? Gone with the wind?' Kriti winked and laughed at what she thought was a joke.

I took in a deep breath and smiled. Kriti's words did not affect me. Rather, I pitied her. She had spent all her life like a frog in the well. She couldn't see anything beyond her rigid ideas of how humans are supposed to live.

'Hi! I'm Neha,' said Neha, stepping forward. 'I don't know who you are, but you need to know something. Energy Healing has helped me. Spiritual practices have helped me. These practices are something that everyone can learn and understand. Even someone like you. But it requires a lot of faith and hard work. It requires you to let go of control. You are afraid of it, right?'

Kriti stared at her with wide eyes.

Neha continued, 'Your mean words are coming from a place of fear. You have lived your entire life believing that only one way of living is right. So, when you saw Aashi doing something unconventional, you felt scared. She was threatening all your beliefs. And Aashi knows that as well. That's why she is still smiling and accepting you into her space.

Kriti gulped aloud and walked away.

Neha turned to me and asked, 'Coffee at your favourite place?'

'Neha, do you know that you are the most understanding

person I have ever met?'

As we sipped into our cold coffees, we remembered our first meeting at Sonal's wedding.

Neha said, 'Look at you now! You have bloomed into this self-confident person who is manifesting her reality.'

I smiled. 'Not just me, Neha. You have become this independent woman who is starting her own business! Just a few months ago you were crying over losing a job. I told you that once you let go of the control, life will happen to you naturally.'

'But I wish your friends didn't treat you that way.'

'Neha, I have realised something. What we see in others is a reflection of ourselves. Maybe, they saw me as a failure because that's how they felt deep inside. It is a projection, you know. They couldn't accept my way of living because it brought up their hidden insecurities. I hope that they seek happiness within.'

Neha raised a toast, and said, 'Cheers to freedom! We have finally gained freedom from control, freedom from criticisms, and freedom from judgments!'

As our glasses clinked, I said, 'Now, life comes to us with ease and joy.'

Found and Lost

Hrishikesh Mokashi

You think you would know a person well after interacting regularly with them during the span of an entire year. However, this may not be the reality always. Communication, the simplest and yet the most profound of all skills, often becomes your worst enemy. It is this skill, or some might prefer to call it an art, which differentiates us from others in the animal kingdom. Humans are "superior" because of this much abused, little acknowledged, insignificant virtue.

These were the thoughts that scribbled through Kumar's minds when he sat today with his diary. Too many life experiences pushed the young mind of Kumar into vivid epiphanies that he now carries along with him, cherishes them, and carefully jots them down in his favourite blue diary. He has always been so sensitive, which others have often taunted him for. Yet, this nature of his is what he cannot help. Hence, the diary where he pours himself out eventually became his best-friend in quite literal sense.

Prolific idioms and wise sayings expound the importance of words: Be careful what you say, for you never take it back. Words fly out swifter than an arrow and the pain and anguish, the heartbreak they cause, is much more wounding than any physical pain an actual arrow would inflict. Many people suffer from 'foot in the mouth' which is infamously known to afflict our bovine brethren. Notorious victims of this plague are our politicians, who often shoot off their mouths, without first considering the implications and the serious ramifications of their asinine comments. Many retractions, insincere apologies and threatened slander and libel cases, thereafter, don't seem to make them realise their folly and they keep committing the same blunder repeatedly.

Apart from politicians, youngsters in particular seem to have a predilection for this problem. Unwittingly at times, they fall prey, in reverse to the common adage that 'Sticks and stones may break my bones, but words can never harm me.' They assume it is their God-given right to speak tactlessly and arrogantly at any given time. Without sparing so much as a thought to what the receiver of their words may feel, they speak the words having the macabre potential. It is possible that they are too naive and uncouth to fully realise the repercussions of their thoughtless words, and yet, the benefit of the doubt is not something to be considered always.

Continuing with his pen and thoughts, he was wondering so many things that are often kept unheard and unsaid. There are way too many things that Kumar simply keep latent in his heart, which, at the end of the day, find place into his blue diary pages—his only confidante.

Speaking one's mind fearlessly is always to be encouraged in the youth but not at the expense of another person's dignity or peace of mind. The humiliation and angst caused to others by their 'blunt speak' is irrevocable and often it causes a needless rift in relationships. Among their peers, they are supposed to take their casual insults and at times the abusive language, in their strides and reciprocate in kind. In fact, 'Give as good as you get' should have been their guiding principle. The same cannot be said when it comes to the interactions between youngsters and adults. The obvious generation gap aside, the callous attitude and the irreverent demeanour of youngsters is enough to arouse the irk of elders and any invaluable advice doled out to them is like water of a duck's back. They are impervious and blissfully oblivious, plainly incapable of paying heed to anything that's said in their best Interests. Everything that's said seems 'disgusting' to them and beneath contempt. In such cases silence can speak volumes.

Silence—something that Kumar had acquired as a skill as he has been growing up, and still learning to be at comfort with it. While his lungs often burst out to speak and yell and express, he soon realised that there was no one at the end of the spectrum who would lend an ear to his ramblings—yes, the ramblings in quite literal sense to everyone else—things that don't make any sense. But sensitivity is what is scarce in the environ he inhabits is what Kumar realised soon enough as he navigated his ways through life… life happened rather too soon to him, and he is the kind of the soul who doesn't know what to do when life gives you lemons—whether to make a lemonade out of them or rejecting them altogether. In between confusion, and the indomitable urge to express, silence seemed to be the obvious path to him—the option that befell upon him on its own with no one around to actually hear his heart out.

Unfortunately, youngsters today are too jaded and their 'Been there, done that' attitude prevents them from appreciating the subtler nuances of life and relationships. This is indeed an alarming trend being witnessed increasingly the world over. It takes away the pleasure and enjoyment of the simpler things in life. The ever-increasing allure of all things material is what drives them and their lives. Everything else is belittled and scoffed at, not being worth their while. Instant gratification is the order of the day. Apart from their narcissistic tendencies, which comes with the territory viz. Adolescence, they can be megalomaniacs who are effortlessly condescending the lesser mortals—their "elders", adding to this is alarming "mood swings", making them chameleons with ever changing colours and we have a very potent, lethal, and explosive concoction in our hands.

Perhaps, it would be unfair to have a one-sided perspective of this issue. It is widely believed that with age comes wisdom. That is again a topic of heated debate. There are many instances to prove that the youth do possess wisdom, intelligence, and sensitivity. In fact, surveys indicate that teenagers are quite capable of taking decisions on their own and don't want or need constant parental guidance or molly coddling. They are often independent and don't require constant reassurance about their abilities. They are focused, goal oriented and often work hard to achieve their goals. Driven by the burning ambition to succeed in their aspirations for life, they are often ruthless and selfish. Showing aside anything or anyone who appears in their path or who seems to be impeding in their progress, they occlude and thwart any attempt to reach them and any overtures are brusquely and off-handedly brushed off. This desire to excel is laudable, yet when it takes control and possesses one to the extent of being insensitive and cruel towards others who care, it ceases to be appealing.

This is a wake-up call to all those who have these delusions of grandeur and who are sated with the heady intoxication of youth. It is never too late to turn over a new leaf. Drop your nonchalant arrogance and be sensitive to the feelings of others around you. You'll discover a brand-new world, one of which is more meaningful and fulfilling as compared to the one you inhabit now. Never forget that the exhilarating days are fleeting. Spend them wisely, for knowledge comes, but wisdom lingers. What was found so fortuitously and serendipitously should be treasured and never lost under any circumstances. Shakespeare's words of wisdom sum it up in a nutshell. 'There is a tide in the affairs of men, which taken at the flood, leads on to fortune. Omitted, all the voyage of their life is bound in shallows and in miseries. On such a full sea are we now afloat, and we must take the current when it serves, our lose our ventures.'

As Kumar finished writing, he went to sleep that night knowing that his self is kept safe between those scribbled pages of the diary. Little did he know that his mother, like a doting parent, has always been around to go-through the pages of emotional outbursts. That night was no exception, and while she flipped those pages, she realised that there is nothing new to find but his sensitive young child's vehement expression of emotions that he could never express in the public or even among his own family. A sensitive boy, a sensitive growing-up boy—something that was never encouraged in the family of hyper-masculine environ—something that forms the foundation of Kumar's family. Hence, the boy was a misfit from the day he was born, or was it the day he expressed his emotions unapologetically as a child? It is difficult to remember everything clearly now for Kumar's mother as she herself has been devoid of any emotional exhibit within this family's stringent framework of equating emotions to weakness, especially for boys who would grow up to be men. Kumar's criticism of youngsters or even the elders echo everything that he himself has been facing all this while from his own family—something that his mother could not help him with.

But she has one solace that her son found a way to express—to outpour his feelings—even if that means opening up to an inanimate object. Sometimes all it takes is an outlet to relive yourself and be your own self again—just an outlet—a friend, a family member, or… just some ruffled up pages of a diary. Her sweet little boy had lost himself among the known and living beings only to find his own self amidst the non-living being—the diary.

Past Life Regressions

Hrishikesh Mokashi

Dear Diary,

Life is indeed strange and wondrous. Frequently we rail against our destiny. It seems as if we receive more than our fair share of trials and tribulations. We come across different people in the journey of life. Some are insignificant and others leave a huge impact. At that very particular moment in time, we don't realise the immense hold that they have over us. What appears to be a fleeting, transient relationship assumes huge proportions later on in life. That's why we use the phrase "ships that pass in the night", often said of the people who meet for a brief but intense moment and then part, never to see each other again. These people are like two ships that greet each other with flashing lights and then sail off into the night. Numerous stories abound about past life regressions or surreal past life experiences. Although we tend to scoff at such stories, what if there was a grain of truth in them somewhere? When you meet people from a past life and the two paths cross, what significance does that have on this life? Many people swear that they have encountered people from their past life and are able to recognise them as such, by the intense feelings that are aroused. If you have a scientific outlook, it is only natural to be sceptical of such stories. In order to understand past life experiences, it is necessary to believe in reincarnation. In the religious mythology of China souls are prevented from remembering their past lives by the deity Meng Po, also known as the "lady of forgetfulness" who gives them a bittersweet drink that erases all memories before they climb the wheel of reincarnation. We have heard of love at first sight or inexplicable hatred for no apparent reason. Now there could well be an explanation for the same. Has there ever been someone in your life whom you reacted strongly to, that you couldn't stand? Or someone you were drawn towards? That reaction is a response to something that the person represents within you, and it may seem magnified many times. Sometimes, some people appear to be anachronisms, a throwback to an earlier period of time. The people we bring into our lives offer us a place to reflect on ourselves, who we are and what we want to accomplish. Our outer world and its relationships are a mirror of our inner world and our relationships with ourselves. That person you are reacting to has come into your life for some reason. The two of you are together, no matter how brief the time, for your mutual experiencing. Everything that happens in our lives happen for a purpose, for a reason and although we may question the wisdom of our actions at times. All that we do affects us and helps to shape us into the individuals that we are. After all, experience is not what happens to us; it is what we do with what happens to us. When we are born, we are endowed with two gifts, our own individuality and free will.

Free will is our ability to make choices and we make thousands of choices each day. Even if we choose not to believe in past life recollections, the decisions we make today will affect our tomorrow. Life in its entirety is very complex and at times indecipherable and incomprehensible. It is therefore imperative to develop an attitude of gratitude and give thanks for everything that happens to you, knowing that every step forward is a step towards achieving something bigger and better than your current situation. Learning to appreciate every little thing that you receive, as a gift from God and understand that God has his purpose, mysterious though it may seem, and he always knows what's best for us is something that shall always sail us through the toughest of the times.

Amit closed the diary that he has made a habit to write down in before going to bed every night. It had been so long that he no longer remembered what it was like to be without any support or guidance. The only thing he remembered was the saying of the Father of the Home he was brought up in since he was a little kid, with both his parents passing away in a crash. He can't even recollect how and what things actually went on at that point of time, neither does he remember the moment he arrived in the Home, which truly became the only "home" he knew ever since.

While growing up amidst the humdrums of the typical establishment that "cared for" the unprivileged and also the "unlucky" ones, Amit was exposed to the brutal side of the life pretty young. Just into his 20's, he penetrated into the world of a more complex nature… the urge to survive… or rather, the fight to survive. To get a job, to get a "home", to get a "family" … the to-do-list was ticked with endless pointers. But whenever he opened his diary after or during reflecting inside himself, he pretty well understood that all of these are mere reflections of what he sees around and is not the reality of what he craves out of the life. What does he actually want from his life? Really, what does he want? He has often pondered over this question whenever he has peeped around and seen the "neighbours" with "happy families", the blood connecting one person to the another, and with him, it has never been the case and he is highly unsure about whether it will ever be like that. He sees and wonders whether he will ever have a "family" of his own… people to call his own… what does it take to have a "family of one's own"?

But in all such tumultuous moments, when he feels helpless and confused about what should be the next way forward… what does he actually craves out of this life, the words of Father become his only companion, 'Have faith in God for he knows what's best for you.'

Standing today, with a well-earning job and his wife and son waiting to welcome him back home as he returns from yet another abroad official trip, he manages to smile through it all… yes, he has managed to smile through it all and has been successful to build a "family" of his own… "people" to call his own… a house that is not only brick and mortar but also a "home" and the home filled with warmth, merry, and laughter echoing from its many corners. Does it have something to do with his past life? Perhaps some good deeds? Who knows!

Reveries in the Silence

Maxine Mathew

There. Finally, a moment of utter peace as I get back to myself and gather up my scattered thoughts.

Grace lies in her cot sleeping like an angel without a care in the world as if the past two hours of crying had never existed. The air still lies heavy with the echoes of her cries. I had paced up and down the room cradling her in my arms, my head filling with nothing else other than her cries. Sometimes in those moments I feel myself slipping away, becoming a hollow shell of a person, just filled with the inconsolable cries of my daughter.

I wonder if this is how my mother felt. This feeling of slipping away, this hollowness. As if the pieces of my identity had been shattered and each time that I tried to gather up these pieces, a tiny little piece was left behind, leaving behind an emptiness.

My memories of my mother are blurred by the passing of time, as if I am looking at her from afar from an unfocussed lens. If I did not have the few photos as a reference, her face, her form would have faded away too. All that is left of her with me are just scattered snippets of memories and a vague feeling of who she was.

In all the memories of my mother, I just remember her as someone sucked of all life. There was no joy, no happiness, no warmth that I associated with my mother. She was like a living ghost. I remember finding her often staring blankly at nothingness, with a forgotten task near at hand.

Perhaps the only time she felt human to me in those distant memories of mine are where she was crying. That is the bit of my memory of my mother that I had clung on to. A little reminder of her, not as a hollow shell of a person, but as someone capable of feeling the depths of human emotion. Yet her crying was not loud. It was almost silent, even though you could see it shaking up her entire body.

My memory of her crying was always in this little room. I have forgotten the purpose of that room, but I think it became my mother's sanctuary. In my memory, she sat crying at one corner of that room, making herself as small as possible as if willing herself to melt away from the suffering of this world. I don't think I ever entered that room as if entering that room would snatch away the last thread of my mother's life. I think I just peaked in from the threshold, curious at this glimpse of my mother's humanity.

I have had these bouts of crying too. I would love to say that it started after Alex chose to move out of the house I had once hoped would be filled with love and laughter, but it had started much before. Even before the marriage I had thought perfect started unravelling, these sudden episodes of inconsolable grief overtook me. Alex usually stood nearby, wringing his hands. He seemed almost afraid to touch me as if I would shatter with his touch or worse that I shall transfer this feeling of desolation and hopelessness to him. He tried to understand this grief, but I was never able to explain the reason for this heaviness in my heart that made me feel isolated from life itself.

These bouts of crying were usually followed by a period of listlessness. The world seemed devoid of hope and meaning in these moments as a darkness took over the life I had built with Alex. These periods passed by, and Alex was usually waiting for me at the other end, patient, worried, and finally relieved for the upcoming period of normalcy.

I had clung on to Alex like he was my life raft, desperately clinging on to his bright light of hope and optimism. I had felt like I belonged with Alex, with his warmth and with his happiness. His inescapable intense yet loving gaze filled me with nervous anticipation and yearning. He had this way of looking at me like I was a puzzle that he was trying to decipher, putting my soul together piece by piece. I felt myself step slowly out of the shadows and finally take the form of a living breathing creature with hopes and dreams.

Before Alex, for as long as I remembered, I had strived to remain invisible. Barely heard. Barely seen. Barely existing. I had tiptoed around my childhood home, not wanting to confront the relatives that filled the house with the inconvenient truth about my sex that was undesired and that encumbered them with responsibilities that they were unwilling to shoulder. Thus, I lived in the crevices of life, watching the world of adults from the shadows, and watching my mother wither away.

My mother's death seemed almost inevitable as she let go of the land of living bit by bit. Death had finally come calling and she had embraced him, happy to finally relinquish her state of half existence. No one told me how she had died. On the day they had found my mother, someone had finally remembered me and told me that she was no more. No further explanation was offered. All I had was snatches of overheard conversation where they called her death shameful, selfish, and aggravating, with exclamations of how my father was finally free of a burden.

My father, still living, seems to be as enigmatic a figure as my mother. In my early childhood, when my mother was still alive, he was a figure I had seen reclining on the wooden rocking chair in the veranda with a newspaper on his hand, sometimes reading, sometimes sleeping with the newspaper moving up and down on his stomach as he inhaled and exhaled. He presents such a stereotypical image in my early memories of him that I sometimes wonder if I have made it all up to fill in his absence later on in my life. After my mother's death, he had quickly found a young new bride, shifted to a new house, and started a new family. I was left behind in the house abounding with relatives that felt no affinity towards me.

My father appeared in my life once a year from then. With each of his appearance, I was snatched from the shadows by some relative, put in my Sunday best, and presented to him for his appraisal. He usually asked if I was not being a trouble and if I was paying attention to my studies. Satisfied with my monosyllabic answers, he used to dismiss me with a grunt as he dealt with the rest of his kin before disappearing for another year. This annual ritual was the extent of our relationship till I eloped with Alex. After that I was consciously erased from my family's memories, with my father refusing to acknowledge me as his daughter.

None of this had mattered as I had Alex. Alex with his kind eyes and disarming smile. Alex, for whom I had stepped into the land of the living after circling its peripheries for years. With Alex, for the first time in my life I felt what it meant to feel hopeful and to be loved. It was an electrifying feeling that I was terrified of losing as soon as I had found it.

Perhaps it was the fear of losing this wonderful gift of hope that had led to my periods of despair and depression. These periods of anguish became increasingly frequent as time passed and lasted for longer. Alex's kindness and patience slowly started ebbing, being replaced in turn by irritation and anger. Like a self-fulfilling prophecy, my fear of losing Alex had seemingly pushed him farther and farther away.

I was on the verge of losing Alex when we got our first news of the pregnancy, and everything seemingly changed overnight. Alex was once again kind and caring, hyper-attentive to my needs. He was buzzing with a happy energy as he looked forward to welcoming our child. I, on the other hand, felt none of the blissfulness or optimism that expecting mothers are supposed to feel. I was horrified as I felt the child slowly grow within my body, unable to prevent it. Yet, I put on a happy face as I saw Alex's joyous mood at the expected arrival of our child. The child became my hope for happiness and my hope for keeping Alex.

Keeping up the masquerade was becoming more and more difficult with each passing day, however, and the mask of bravado and happiness I had put on for months broke after the birth. Grace's birth had been excruciating and after the pain when I was handed her fragile body, I felt none of the love that a new mother is supposed to feel. Instead, I was gripped with terror at her frailty and mortality. In the months that followed I switched between hyper-vigilance and a catatonic state; almost forgetting Alex's existence as I lived for Grace, afraid of losing her the moment I shut my eyes.

It was during one of the increasingly frequent fights with Alex where he talked about being isolated from his daughter and being trapped in an unhappy marriage that I had screamed, 'Then go!' Alex was taken aback for a minute and then like I had provided him with a new lease of life, he took the escape I had provided him. We negotiated custody, as Alex again became the picture of understanding, agreeing to give me primary custody of our daughter for her first few years. And then it was over. The relationship that had given me the first glimpse of hope and love was reduced to the exchange of a few courteous words every other week when he came to pick up our daughter for the weekends.

So, here, I am. Alone, with my daughter, Grace, in the house that was once bustling with expectation. My mind keeps going back to my mother more frequently nowadays as I struggle to prevent the state of unbecoming that I most remember my mother in. I struggle to remain afloat for my daughter, instead of letting go. However, darkness seems to be gaining pace inch by inch. But, for now, a sense of calm permeates my being as Grace sleeps, and all is well.

Mental Games

Neeraja Krishnaswami

Below is a situation of calm and conflict where a young girl named Manyaa, is musing to her mind.

Or you can say, talking or replying to what are her innermost fears in life in the form of a dialogue with her mind or inner soul.

A place where she was peddling her way through peaks and troughs!

A little background here!

The girl had been brought up very protectively and received everything from her family before she even asked for it.

Yet, she felt the spice in her life was missing.

Why did she feel so or what circumstances led her to think that way? That is what this piece is about.

So why wait?

Let's get on with the soliloquy, which ultimately ends with conclusive thought.

Manyaa: Hi there!

Yes, I had a past, of that terrible mental ailment, so debilitating it is!

Till date, I have haunted thoughts about it.

Mind: That is past. What are you getting at?

Manyaa: Yeah, I know, I know.

Coming to today's topic.

Firstly, having medication for being sane is not a downcast on me, I choose to believe.

And second, two days ago, by being distraught yet subtle, my father indicated to me that I need to take responsibility and that he is feeling like giving up and enjoying every moment of his life that is remaining, something which is out of his hands, he feels, at the moment.

I know, I know. You would say that both points are true!

So true that I feel morally responsible at times for everything!

Mind: You should. And why not?

Manyaa: How's that of any validation?

Why being content is important, is something I think about nowadays.

I am thinking about something to give my life a sense and direction, some aim of mine, which I want to dream and live for, as my father is alive and he sees the bright day that I will face, while being confident and content, and being able to take sensible decisions, without me having to take my father's handholding for granted.

Mind: This is something any daughter or son may feel.

Manyaa: Only, the difference being, me being expressive through my writing, about this fact.

Mind: And?

Manyaa: Yes, you guessed right. There is an "and".

Another situation I had to face today, after the sunset, was my father telling me that I have no brains! Now, tell me, even a person with Alzheimer's Disease—once remembered important things, as did a person who was christened brilliant—courtesy his topper status in student life.

So, if both these situations have happened, even a person with a mental ailment can have brains!

Mind: True. Go on!

Manyaa: So then, my getting upset, yet not shedding a single tear, after hearing this about me, is evidence enough that I have grown up!

Even after listening to this, I remained calm.

Do you get it?

Mind: Entirely.

But it is not over yet—or is it?

Manyaa: The last pangs of depression in me saw the daylight when I had my menstrual cycle this month.

And before that cycle, I was down for 2 days! 48 hours!

Can you believe it?

Mind: Kind of.

What's your take?

Manyaa: My take is somewhat like this.

When the cycle began, it was not a blissful one, yet it was manageable.

On the second day of my menstrual cycle, I got vaccinated for COVID-19.

And after the cycle died, and the vaccination after-effects subsided, came out a different, calmer, sensible version of me, a version that I, myself, was very sceptical and unaware about, and that I thought would never be coming out anytime soon!

After that, I am still going strong and having a whirlwind of thoughts in my head, some exquisite, new, and fresh, while others twitched with a pang of satisfaction, realisation and understanding.

But there is hope before and after everything.

Mind: Hope is the eternal solace-giving factor in life.

For if there is no hope, there is no faith or future.

Manyaa: Yes, but…

Mind: But you have questions, don't you?

Want to have a question-and-answer session? For better clarity or vision?

Manyaa: Yes, thank you, please do!

Do note, here, the questions asked, belong to the state of mind of the person who is in question, not of the mind.

Getting on with the session!

Mind: Will this new version of me last?

Manyaa: I don't know!

Mind: Will this version of me, take me to larger horizons?

Manyaa: I don't know!

Mind: Will this be a turning point in my life?

Manyaa: Maybe, not so sure.

Mind: But am I sure about making myself great in my own eyes?

Manyaa: YES.

Mind: Will my family understand this version of me?

Manyaa: Again, a maybe.

Mind: Will my family support me?

Manyaa: Yes, or maybe.

Mind: Will I be able to relieve my parents of their responsibility?

Manyaa: Can't say.

Mind: But you can't snatch away from your parents their right of wishful thinking about making and witnessing the growth-graph of the youth and adulthood of their first-born daughter, can you?

Manyaa: The situation is terrible, but we need to face it, as a family.

I need to face it, by virtue of being an integral part of my family.

Not saying that it is an easy road to tread on, to embark upon, but still, acknowledging some truths and facts needs to be done!

Ending this question-and-answer session and coming to what she learnt from this.

Manyaa was still in her deep thoughts. She noted a lot many things through this ongoing conversation with her own mind, which are now kind of rushing through her—something she can feel in her nerves…

All the time we have with us is between the day we were born and till the day we die. Whatever we are in the intervening timespan, is what we are. I don't know whether we have seven lives or not. But what I know is we have this life. This one life. So, shouldn't we live it to the fullest? Living life to the fullest does not always mean living materialistically but living with calmness and contentment. Some people realise this later and some sooner. Ask yourself, which category do you fit into? Situations can be of two types—one, Internal i.e., within ourselves and two, external i.e., with the outside world. In the past few years, I have faced a lot of situations. All of us must have faced a lot of situations. Some good, some bad. Some with satisfaction and others with dissatisfaction. But does that mean we stop living? We live and continue living no matter what. The Business Cycle in the subject Economics that she had studied, as she remembered, spoke of 4 Phases—Recovery, Prosperity, Recession and Depression. After Recovery and Prosperity, a business reaches its Peak. Similarly, after Recession and Depression, a business reaches its Trough. And the cycle continues. Her thoughts further strolled on wandering that in a hospital, when a patient is in a critical condition, he is put on life support, you can spot an ECG machine showing electrical signals of the beating of the heart. If the heart beats, the machine shows ups and downs, it means that person is alive. If the machine shows a single horizontal line, it means that person is dead. So, it is important that the heart beats.

All situations affect us. If something happens and it makes

us happy, we feel positive. On the other hand, if something happens which makes us weep and feel sad or angry, we brand it as negativity immediately. But isn't this what life throws at us? Agreed that every person faces and copes with situations differently. Not every person will face the same situation. And since every situation is different, the problems faced are different, each person will have their own way of dealing with it uniquely.

Manyaa is now composed than ever, at peace with herself, embracing the realities of her life, accepting herself the way she is. Such episodes of her and her mind often connect her to her inner self she believes, ultimately helping her to take a step forward toward something better in terms of understanding her own self, her surroundings, the people she loves. Every situation is a test, she reminded herself, now with a smile on her face… a smile that reflected content, as her thoughts kept telling her, 'If we sail through it, we feel we have achieved victory. But if we do not and get stuck in between, it does not mean that we should succumb to it, it just means that we are a little farther away from reaching the shore. We are ultimately going to reach the shore, yes, but in this journey, we gain a lot of experience. Someone once told her, when she was in a deep low regarding not being able to pursue my career in the way she had charted out for myself, that it is the effort that matters and not the result. So, life is not life if it doesn't have its share of peaks and troughs. Learn to live with contentment (and not pride) during your peaks and sail without taking stress during the troughs.'

Awaiting Afterlife

Vaishnavi Tawade

How are you feeling papa?

My daughter asked her ailing old man, knowing well the time to go is near.

I, her dearest papa, lay on the bed with my random thoughts brimming across the brain and heart, feeling excruciating pain in every sense but literal. Filled with the thoughts of afterlife, I waited, patiently, to be arrived at the gates of the heaven or hell, whatever awaits me. But so many things simply keep coming back to me at the moment. The past, the present that is the past now, and the present that does not have any future.

Things come with expiry dates; they perish in given time. But it is only the human soul that seeks aspiration for an immortal journey, I wonder why. Maybe the mortal sufferings stretch every inch of its living existence towards delusionality, wanting more. Is there something more even? I believe, yes. All my life I have seen human sufferings in different shapes and forms, their complexity, so intestine twisting that I would rather want to be born as an insect. In this mucky world, I'd rather be a mortal dead. But in the other world, where there lies immortal bliss, I shall sway away.

I remember my wife's death. I saw her scorching pain with my own two eyes, until that very moment. That moment when suddenly her bodily anguish dissolved cold, she slept peacefully. As much as I resented every ounce of the sufferings that occurred to her, her sudden blissful repose hushed my rambling mind. I felt peace, through her peace. I wondered when my time comes, will I submit myself in unfinished chaos or a kind of bliss that is unknown to the mortals. My thoughts about death grew deeper like a deep dark forest, and every day I felt like I was getting swallowed into the darkness. I knew my time was close, I felt sensitive even to thin air.

My feet ran cold as I sat on my green fleece chair, the thoughts of my nearing death making me feel blue. The aches in my body dissolving frantically with the aches in my heart. Looking over from the windowsill I saw my daughter waving me goodbye, she was leaving from her two-hour visit, leaving her dying father. In those two hours, I could barely speak to her about the melancholic chaos within me. My lips felt heavy, not a single word birthing from my mouth. I wondered that even if I would be able to phrase my emotional frenzy, would she understand? I think not. Only a dying old man like me would understand how the presumptions of death have haunted my mind. Afterall, death is not a painful process, but the thoughts of death are. The thoughts about death were like thorns studded on a beautiful rose. They kept pricking me, sharper than ever now. That the thoughts about death harrow deeper than the bodily aches. Those demons have infested me, how these thoughts have phased the last moments of my living. I had no idea where I was going to go but it was sure the time was close, and the clock was ticking louder than ever for me…my life was ending. I had nobody with me, just the thoughts of my ending life and me. My after life was waiting for me as I felt my flesh turn cold, I could feel it get into me, giving me whiffs of its impending arrival. I could feel my soul being sucked out of my worn-out body, my soul scratching the outlines of my skin. My soul was now hovering around my ice-cold body, it felt light. I was outside of what cased my soul, I didn't know where to go. Looking below I saw my daughter and rest of my family solemnly standing around me, behind me were all my ancestors floating lightly through with a light beaming glow. They were waiting for me in a place where there was extreme serendipity, where all my living chaos dissolved dead. I wanted to free my thoughts, there was no brain jittery now, there was no need of it now. I wanted to reconcile with my dead forebearers, I knew they had undone chaos too, I wondered why they still looked calm and bona fide. I saw the glistening glow of their souls. They didn't need resolution, they already achieved it. My death felt like the only pathway to freedom, freedom from the living chaos. Afterlife had opened his arms wide for me, embraced me mystically, peacefully. I was there, I was right there, it was the first time that I felt free and floaty. I never really waited for this moment, but my soul was longing for it. I longed for my other life… my afterlife.

You Are Never Alone

Hiya Banerjee

'Olivia is a good girl! It is impossible for her to have bullied you! Stop lying for God's sake!' Rylie's grandmother's words echoed around the room.

'I haven't been lying to you!' Rylie shouted; tears were in her eyes; but she tried to look brave.

Grandmother sighed, 'Think of it as you want, but one thing is clear; they were just playing with you, Rylie.' Saying this, she walked out the door.

Rylie pressed the meat of her hands to her eyes to keep from crying again and thought, *if only mother…* She pinched her hand and said to herself, 'It's okay, even if mother isn't here, I'll try my best and see what I can do on my own.' She reluctantly descended the stairs, smiling but unsure what to say. After trying a number of times, she ended up saying that she is going for a walk.

She went towards the park and that is when she noticed people sitting in a gaming zone across the street. They cheered and chatted. They looked so alive. She wanted to cross the street and join them just to connect with them—to be a part of something. But a subtle voice that came from within, that whispered from the open wounds in her heart, held her back from doing so. She kept walking, alone.

The next afternoon while Rylie was going down the alley—back home from school, she ran into a girl with silky blonde hair and chocolate brown eyes. Olivia! Rylie gasped in horror. 'It's you! Can't you see where you are walking!' Olivia bawled.

Rylie started, 'I am sorry I didn't mean to…' But before Rylie could finish, Olivia took out her water bottle and threw cold water on Rylie. 'You ran into me first and then I poured water on you, we are even now,' she said and walked past Rylie. Rylie wanted to shout back at her, but something wouldn't let her speak; something inside her knew that if she spoke now, her grandparents would blame her for something she didn't do. So, Rylie decided to let it pass and go home. It didn't take long for Rylie to get home, and as soon as she entered from the front door, she was scolded harshly by her grandmother for playing around with water. Saddened by the rebuke, Rylie went upstairs to her room and took a nice warm bath. She just wanted to relax for a while that is when she heard footsteps which slowly creaked on every step of the stairs. The door handle turned slowly. Her hair stood on end, a shiver raced down her spine and a lump came to her throat. It was him… her grandfather, Mr. Calvin Quinton. Not only did he return home early, but Olivia Wilson was also there with him!

Mr. Quinton asked, 'Do you know why she is here?' to

which Rylie replied 'Yes, I do.'

'Do you know what you did wrong?' he asked.

'But Grandfather, I didn't do anything wrong, it was just a misunderstanding,' Rylie protested.

Mr. Quinton looked at Olivia, but Olivia lied, 'Mr. Quinton, she really did push me and then…'

'She's lying!' Rylie shouted.

Mr. Quinton calmy asked, 'Then how do you explain this?'

Olivia touched her thumb to a wound on her knee and hissed.

'I didn't,' replied Riley.

'You didn't do it? Then how did she get hurt like this! You are going too far with your lies Rylie!' Her grandfather's angry voice was accompanied by a slap. Though she didn't want to cry in front of him, Rylie started crying. She gazed up into his angry red face and said, 'I know that you don't trust me, but I hope you will at least believe it to be possible.' She pushed Olivia away from the door and ran downstairs, exasperated. There was a loud bang as the front door slammed at Rylie's violent departure.

Without a second thought she ran up to the grassy hill where the garden of remembrance was located, she wanted to see her parents. When Rylie reached the crest, it was covered with wildflowers; it was a beautiful sight. Rylie laid a picture of her and her mother and knelt beside her mother's grave closing her eyes. A few minutes later she looked up smiling and said, 'Mother, I have been doing well, I have been eating well too and recently I have taken a liking towards reading different kinds of books but…' the smile on her face faded, 'to be honest, reading isn't what I really want. What I really want is for someone—anyone at all—to tap me on my shoulder and invite me into their world. To ask me questions and tell me stories. To understand me. To laugh with me. To want me to be a part of their life. I really want this, but no one believes me, everyone thinks that I am a liar! But I have never lied, not even once.' The stored tears continued to flow, and the sobs wracked her body, robbing it of the ability to speak—barely allowing a breath to be drawn.

It was already dark; Rylie knew she had to return home before it gets too late, but she didn't want to. At that very moment when she stood up, icy fingers gripped her arm in the darkness. Rylie shrieked in fear and pushed away the icy hand that was gripping her. The boy hit the ground with a thud and groaned.

'Back off!' Rylie shouted while taking a step backwards.

'Come on! There's no need to yell at me!' the boy shouted back. He stood up and brushed of the dust from his clothes, he had high cheekbones and caramel bushy hair with grey eyes. He looked up at Rylie and smiled. 'I didn't think I'd find someone else roaming around here during the dark hours.' But Rylie still looked uncomfortable, she looked like she immediately wanted to run away. The boy noticed this and said, 'Well, I think even I would've freaked out if someone touched me without me noticing. So, to make you feel better let me introduce myself, I am Warren Davis, nice meeting you.' By introducing himself, Warren seemed to have mollified Rylie. 'I live near the church, where do you live? And why are you alone when it's already dark?' Warren asked. 'Can I trust you?' Rylie asked. 'You can tell me, rest assured I won't do anything to harm you,' Warren promised. Rylie took a deep breath and said, 'I ran away from home.' As soon as Warren heard this he burst into laughter. Rylie looked at him irritated.

'I am sorry I didn't mean to, but you just don't look so old that you could run away from your home and come all the way up here,' said Warren while trying to catch his breath.

'Hey! I am 15 already!' Rylie cried out.

Recovering from the laugh Warren asked, 'So why did you run away?'

'I had a fight with my grandfather,' she replied.

'So, you ran away from home; that's foolish,' said Warren.

Well, for me it's more than a foolish act, usually it gets lonely out there all by myself, it's better to hide than stay at a place where you are called a liar when you never really lied,' said Rylie with a slight smile.

Warren looked at her with empathy in his eyes. 'My parents died when I was 10 and since then I have lived with my grandparents', Rylie continued. 'I have often been bullied by kids for being quiet and boring especially by a girl called Olivia Wilson. She was the best at everything, but I turned out to be better than her when it came to academics, so she disliked me. Not only did she mistreat me she even lied to my grandparents and claimed that I was the one who bullied her!'

'So, you never told your grandparents the truth?' Warren asked.

'I did! I did everything I could to make them understand the truth, but they never believed me! They always decided to choose Olivia over me!' Rylie yelled.

'And what about others? Did you ever reach out to others for help or opened up so that you could understand which person would help you and trust you?' Warren questioned.

'I—I never tried! I was scared, I thought it'd just be a waste to ask for someone else's help. I am sure everyone around me thinks I am just useless person who will burden them,' Rylie said while avoiding eye-contact with Warren.

Warren sighed and said, 'Look I don't know what could make you feel better but understanding the situation, all I can say to you is, whatever happens to you, don't take it personally... Nothing other people do is because of you. It is because of themselves.'

Rylie looked up, tears welling up in her eyes.

Warren looked straight at her and said, 'You are never alone, okay? Someone somewhere cares about you and wants you to be alright, even if it's just a random person you met on the internet. You are loved. Don't forget that.'

Rylie nodded. It was something she had been hoping to hear, something she had been waiting for all this time. Her chest clenched as she began to cry again. At that moment she was happy. For the first time she experienced a warm, dark, autumn night.

The First Meet

Srija Sanyal

*I hold it true, whate'er befall; I feel it, when I sorrow most;
'Tis better to have loved and lost Than never to have loved
at all.*

ALFRED TENNYSON

'Are you sure about this?'

'Absolutely.'

'I really don't want to end up like a person whom you just slept with. I want myself to mean something in your life Ani. Without it, this would mean nothing.'

Few days have passed since the realisation of falling for Ani has dawned upon Srikanya. It all started with a genuine mutual admiration and healthy flirting. The very first steps taken by Ani on expressing his feelings... how was it though? When did it ever happen? Srikanya can't remember clearly. It has been over 5 years now. And at that time, she hardly paid any heed. What she remembers instead, though blurred, is telling Ani that it will get over soon… it is just a phase… he will be over it soon. Srikanya smiles. It is something she tells herself repeatedly these days. Like a child consoled by the mother in her laps… '*It will be alright… it will be ok… everything will be alright. Strong girl. Strong Sri.*'

Srikanya at times wonders what exactly it is that she lacks. A good husband, a fine job… she has it all. But whether she wanted it or not and how she wanted it, is really the question. Sitting in the office chair she is right now inking the words running through her mind. She wanted to write. She always wanted to write as far as she can remember. She used to be such a vibrant soul. Focused. Hopeful. Now, neither the vibrance nor the focus or hope is there. They all decided to evade her all at once!

'What do you want, Sri?'

'I want to be free Ani. Like free… in the real sense. I don't want to be backed down by the circumstantial compulsions. All these mandates… I don't like them.'

'Then break free.'

'How?'

'Come with me. We can both work here. Work our asses off. Pursue higher studies. Live in small shabby places or may be at bus stations, whichever will be cheaper.'

'And eat what? English bread and jam? And 'rock the bed' at night? Is that your idea?'

'No, Sri. The idea is to never 'rock the bed' but to create memories. We will create memories, Sri. Come with me.'

This was one of the last convos that Sri and Ani had before Anirban Majumder went to pursue his PhD at the

University of Manchester. They never met. It was during one of those days of messy relationships and the struggle to do something in life that there was a message in his Messenger. A post rather. A shared post, about the death of a famous actor. Clearly a forwarded message that has been through many such inboxes, Ani had thought. The sender's name highlighted as Srikanya Sen. But for some reason, Ani clicked on the name to open the profile. And one thing led to another. A short reply from his end opened the gates of endless discussions on the actor and his works, and the state of 'parallel' cinema in India, and what and where Bengal stands amidst this, followed by many how-s and why-s on a diversified spectrum of subjects. On knowing her more and more in the following days, he could not help but admire her spirit to seek knowledge despite all odds that she has faced in her life.

Yes. That was the start. A mutual respect and genuine affection for the pursuer of knowledge. Nothing more, nothing less. Since then, till today. Things are so very different now. They have published works together, presented in seminars. And yet they have never met. It is like the pen friends of the earlier times. Just that now everything is carried on WhatsApp and Google Hangouts.

'You know, I am going to write a book or something of that sort someday. Few people will acquire a significant space in that piece.'

'Yeah, yeah, I get it. You mean I will be one of those "lucky few", right?'

'Yeah. True.' Ani had replied back then with a lopsided smile on his face.

Today, looking back, it all feels so surreal to Srikanya. Ani had said that back then. Today, she is the one writing it all down. What has changed? Too many things perhaps. Her feelings for sure. And his, too. When she actually started to fall for this person, she can't recall now. It is just that she feels so strongly about him right at this moment. And that's what stand as the truth for her. The truth of the present day. He is sitting far away. Too busy… to think, to reply, to feel the unsaid. Between all the sexting, and crying and long hours of video chats, the excitement, the love, the lust… everything… Srikanya stands here today. Feeling for Anirban more than ever, she feels helpless and equally disappointed in herself to be not able to concentrate on her own life. Messaging Ani time and again even with the full knowledge that he will not reply. He has a life. Beyond her. She does not. As if time has ceased to exist beyond that one person. It is absurd, knows Srikanya. Life does not stop for anyone. And she knows she will get over this… once again she will find herself… the self that she loved the most… the self which does not belong to anyone. But today… it stands all so painful for Srikanya. Unbearable. The pain of unrequited love. Right now, while she types down all these a veil of tears is slowly making its way through her eyes. The veil reflects the images of that face, of long conversations, of smile, smoking pipe, the smoke… all blurred within a moment. Tears are now running down the cheeks, keeping pace with the fast fingers that are hitting the keys of the laptop.

They were supposed to meet. Yes. After 5 long years, a meeting was supposed to happen between Sri and Ani. They promised to meet, to see, touch, and feel each other for the very first time. The smell… it was supposed to be unique. Of love, of lust, of longing. But today nothing of the sort is happening. Instead, Ani finds himself alone in the crowd in Delhi, the place where he was supposed to meet his Sri. It is true that he has been busy for the past few months. But it was all because he had to come to Kolkata during the Pujas and had to submit his thesis. He knew Sri needed him… all those constant calls and messages. He could gauge something is going toward the wrong. But he knew his Sri. She is strong. She is brave. She will be fine. He tried to reach out… whenever it was possible for him. He was never an expressive person. He is nothing in front of Sri. She pours her heart out to whom she loves. Her approach to love is unique, appreciable. And he is the one for Sri. Ani could not have felt more honoured. But he could never tell her that over calls… those text messages… the video chats. But all was kept safe within him. And he intended to pour his heart out to her and embrace her and all her insecurities, love. But he is now met with rather a strange news.

He has met her. After all these years, this is finally happening. Only, she is lying in front of him right now. On bed. Wrapped in wires. In a hospital. She committed suicide. Sri, Ani's Sri, committed suicide. Couldn't take all the rejection. Poor soul. Or coward? Ani is still not in his senses. Yet to grasp the body in front of him as his Sri's. His eyes, his soul, still searching for that kiddish face, the mole on the left cheek, the flush of red when she used to see him on video chats. She was supposed to meet him at the airport. He could still visualise her running toward him, a bright face, hugging him tight, their bodies, in contact for the first time. Which is the truth? Ani's mind is in shambles. And so is everything that stood between these two souls in that cold hospital chamber.

At Last

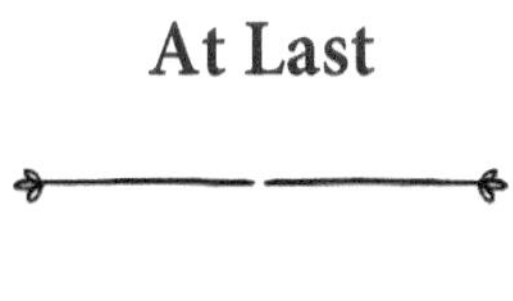

Srija Sanyal

'Are you kidding me?'

'Nope. I am not kidding about having kids.'

'How?'

'Well, you should know it better, shouldn't you, Anish?'

'Huh!'

Anish still cannot believe his ears. Time has come to stop between those two pink lines. Really? Is this for real?

He is happy for sure. But how it's all going to get managed keeps him worried, too. It's unique. The experience. At one moment, he simply wants to fly back to Delhi. His mind is practically taking him back to that hotel room, where he met her for the very first time, where he was bruised, not only his body but his soul. And for once, he had actually cherished those bruises. He still does. Whenever he has looked at that scar on his lips, he is reminded of that one day—the day of absolution of all the longings, yearnings, and love, and lust. She gave herself up completely to him. Oh, how she loved him! He did not know such thing existed before.

It's not that he has not been with women before or has not been in love. But he is a different person now. Once he did dream of setting up a family with a woman. But now, it is all in the past. He has moved on, got a job, pursued his dream, and is teaching now at the university here in London. It is like Ashoke Ganguly from The Namesake, who used to take pride in seeing the nameplate bearing his name in all caps at the door of his room. Filled with books, class schedules, and his dreams, he feels a sense of pride and satisfaction that in his twenties only, he has managed to achieve that nobody in his family back in Kolkata would have dreamt of. It might resemble the feeling of many of those Gangulys and Mukherjees who set afoot in the distant land with dreams in their eyes and the lump of nostalgia in their throats and talk of the magnificence of the coloniser's world upon their return home.

'You still there?'

'Hmm.'

'What "hmm"? Say something. Should I get an appointment?'

'For what?'

'You know for what, *gadha**!'

'Oh, please. Cut the crap, Sri. You know what I want. We talked about this.'

'Are you serious?'

'What do you think?'

'Ani, please. I seriously don't have the time for all these

naekamo* of yours. Why can't you utter clearly?'

Well, yes. That has always been one of the issues in their long-term and long-distance "relationship". He has never been expressive enough, while she has always been with too many expressions. She has been his companion for so many years now. Yes. Many, many years. From texting on the limited balance of message card sitting in the corridors of Presidency to the hotel room of the Imperial few months back. It has been a journey indeed. They often compared themselves as the Snehomoy, and Meyagi, his Japanese wife, who never met but were together in heart and soul. It was indeed a distant dream for them as well. To meet. In person. But it did happen. And it was wonderful. It was wonderful when he adjusted himself in the arch of her back, his knees in the back-arch of hers, while he wrapped his arms around her. He could smell her, the pulse at her neck beating where there is a thin string lies of the necklace that he has just given her. It is all so beautiful, Ani had thought. Time had stopped for him at that moment while he let the moment linger on his senses.

Anish was drawn toward Sri since the very first time they interacted over the internet. Even though he was with someone at that time, he still felt a strong attraction toward Sri. Then, life happened. Drugs, depressions, loads of rejections, and here he is, now. The only constant factor through all these has been Sri. They were never in a "relationship" as such, and they did laugh about the status often in their long hours of video chats. And boy, they discussed what-not. And it did include children, though he was not sure whether it was in humour or on a serious note. But they did decide that if they ever got to meet, and if their rendezvous continued, there was a high probability that this day would come one day. And when it would arrive, they would embrace the "relationship" tag with warmth. And today is that day.

Over one of their many random calls spanning over days and years, Anish says,

'Sri…'

'Hmm.'

'You still there?'

'Yeah. What now?'

'I love you.'

'Oh god, Anish. I already know that. Tell me what to do now.'

'Nothing to do. We will do what we planned.'

'No.'

'What "no"?'

'What do you mean, "we would get married"? And have this kid? And then do songshar* happily ever after? Listen to yourself, Anish! You never wanted to get married or have children. Feeding bottles, wailing babies, diapers, stinking rooms… yuck! These were your words. Now what has happened suddenly?'

'Sri. You know me better than this. I don't want any more arguments on this. I will come during the year end. We will think of something. Don't you want this, Sri? You can come here and stay with me. We can build a world here. Of us. Three.'

'Two and a half, mister.'

'Oh, yes. But it will be three soon. And may be more.'

'Shut up!'

Anish smiles. After quite a while, he is actually feeling happy. Complete. Even after securing a respectable position at the university abroad, life had not seemed to be on track, though he was enjoying the rollercoaster ride. And he yearned, practically always, the absence of that one person, who was sitting there far miles away. And now he can see the family he always dreamt of… a picture taking shape in front of him. He looks at the watch. Time to get up for work. He has to really work hard and earn and save loads of money. Too much to do, too little time. And with that, once again, Anish Mishra walks down the lane toward the university gate. Only this time, he shines even more radiantly than the sun behind him.

*Gadha – asshole

*Naekamo – acting like a fool; intentional pretence

*Snehomoy and Meyagi – lead characters of the novel The Japanese Wife by Kunal Basu where the lead characters enter into a loving conjugal bond while never meeting in reality.

*Songshar – family life

The Realm of Divinity

Hrishikesh Mokashi

Every evening a scientist sat on a bench talking about the surroundings and his research with God. They shared their thoughts, even though they hardly ever matched. Still the scientist could hardly enjoy a day without conversing with him. They always had soft contradictions.

Once, while an interesting talk on love and marriage was going on, a boy about 23 years in age, with a thick science journal shut close in his hands, was walking by, and from the opposite came a beautiful young girl, caught in her own thoughts. The scientist analysed her body language and came to a conclusion that she was a complete stranger. As they crossed each other, they just exchanged a glance and carried forward on their stroll, just with a more widened smile. God asked the scientist whether they would get married or not. The scientist just shook his head sideways saying, 'Nope!'

The next day about the same time, the boy returned but this time the journal was missing, his hair was combed, and a bit of perfume sprayed, and a girl better dressed, walking more as if on a ramp, appeared from the other end of the path. They exchanged a smile and had a brief conversation.

The scientist looked at God in disbelief but did not take his words back.

A few months later, they were spotted again in the park but this time, the boy wearing a black blazer with a bow tie and the girl in a snow-white gown, a perfect bride and groom. The scientist was shocked.

The two strangers met and got married in a few months. He asked God the reason and God replied, 'It's love, my child.'

The scientist grinned and said, 'Love is just a philosophy.'

God replied, 'So am I for many people.' God said that even the scientist would know what love all is about.

The scientist replied, saying, 'Then please explain to me the symptoms of love, so when I do happen to have it, I would be able to identify it.'

God smiled and said, 'There are no such symptoms, but when you see her, your face might turn red, you might have loads of thought, but lack words. You will end up spending more time at the mirror and the main thing is that your heart will start deciding.'

The scientist just acted as if he hadn't heard God's words, waved his hand, and went back to his routine work. While walking back, the scientist saw a beautiful young girl, his brain stopped analysing and his heart started thinking. He could feel his face growing warm, he started sweating a bit, but he had a wide smile and thought to himself, 'Oh, God, I love her!'

The place where facts, theories, logic ends; that is where divine begins.

Poems

The Girl from My Dream

Anurag Pandey

Every day I wake up with a hope in my mind.
That I will see myself in your beautiful shiny eyes.

But your eyes seem to be lost somewhere.
Or it's just an illusion leading my heart to nowhere.

Every night I go to bed with the fear that I might lose you.
What will happen if someone else choose you.

I want to say a lot and I am struggling so hard.
To convey my thoughts about what's going on in my
heart.

Maybe someday you will see the purity of my love.
I will always remain beside you even if the whole world
becomes blurred.

When I see your beautiful shiny eyes.
It reminds me, depth of stars in the sky.

Just want to say don't be always shy.
whole world is waiting for you, you just have to try.

Maybe one day you will understand what I mean.
That for me you will always remain my queen.

When I am with you every moment becomes special.
You are the one with whom I want to settle.

Perpetuity Is a Myth

Aksheeta Chandok

"Perpetuity is a myth," we say.

If we find every story to be identical to ours,

why do they have us circling their name with hearts?

Isn't always and forever what we're praying for?

Yes, we are! So why do we have reservations?

We blame our love and attempt to make a big deal
out of it,

But we all know the problem that lies, is within.

Our generation's flaw is that we have redefined love.

We fall quickly, stop easily, and then lament, claiming that
our story was not written in the heavens above.

We fling "I love you's" like they're nothing special.

As if they're not the three magical words for which the
"forevers" were created.

The phrase's allure appears to have faded.

We are the ones who have failed to remain strong,

yet we blame fate and faith for all that has gone wrong.

Isn't it true that love can strike twice?

Yes, it most certainly can.

But it's the sort of love that only comes around once in a
lifetime,

'The kind of love that cures and never fades away.'

So, whenever you find yourself blaming your partner,

remember that love is pleasant,

Love is an enchanting sentiment.

Love is both sterling and verdant.

It's simply not intended for individuals like us.

The Sky That Holds You

Aksheeta Chandok (Ash)

Today, I smiled warmly as I looked up at the starry sky.

Even though it was bitterly chilly that day, I didn't notice until you approached me.

You leaned down and kissed my forehead, saying, "You have a difficult time expressing yourself, but just gazing into your eyes, I can tell you everything. I can understand the innocence of whatever sentiment you want to communicate, and I will be the only one who understands it till the end. I hope you realise that."

I still miss your heart-melting smile when we were holding hands.

Now I'm sitting here, pondering the beauty of the words
you left for me when you went.

Somewhere inside, I thought I was insane, but I managed
to restrain the shy giggle.

I got your alerts, like I did every day, and felt those
butterflies dance in my stomach, just as they used to when
you were here.

Memories In A Playlist

Aksheeta Chandok (Ash)

Do you still have that one playlist
in your library on my name?

However, even if you do,
I doubt the tunes remained the same.

Do you remember how we used to envision ourselves
as characters in the song?

From dancing in the rain to assuring you that you're the
one person to whom I wanted to belong?

The feelings we exchanged were so pure,

and now I want to miss you but, my heart isn't sure.

I knew the hardest path had begun,

when I heard that one word I couldn't relate with anyone.

From listening to that one tune on repeat to think about
you,

to ignoring that tune to not miss you.

I still want to listen to that playlist and spend the entire
night,

remembering the glorious times that we had and holding
each other tight.

You Don't Know What It's Like to be Me

Hiya Banerjee

You don't know what it's like to be me.

What it feels when people think you are petty.

Sometimes it can even feel ghastly

But in the end, they will think that you have no integrity.

I haven't felt extreme happiness in a while.

I just hope I don't grow heartless in time.

But I would lie if I said my story is unrhymed.

There are many moments when my ecstasy shines.

I am not ready to give up—not just yet.

It is true that there are many memories I want to forget.

However, there are countless which I will never regret.

I no longer want to be upset.

This time, I want to love myself and focus on my present.

Amoretti On Its Way

Srija Sanyal

And so, we lay

Soul to soul

Body to body

Transfixed

Staring the eternity

In each other's gaze

A touch

A sensation

The fire of passion

Shivering through the body

Whereupon you mark

Your own territory

Fingers march past

Crossing lanes

And by lanes

Discovering new arch

Nooks

Leaving your imprints

Of pride

Of affection

Meanwhile I

Twitch and turn

Beneath

In a painful pleasure

Urging cessation

Yet appealing not

As a new self discovers

Chapped lips

Dry and wet

Bruised skin

No pain

Sore body

But rejuvenated soul

The lips part

And merge

An unquenched thirst

Around the navel

The skin catches fire

As your fingers roll over

Igniting a fresh blaze of desire

The firmer it becomes

The soul awakens

As you

Within me

Deepen

Amorous, sensuous

It is hard to tell

Words always fall short

Louder echoes the soul

And so, we lay

Transfixed

You, holding me

Gently

As I unfold

Blooming

Blossoming

And I crumble

You, holding me

Firmly

Cupping me

Entirely

Bare us

Bare bodies

Bare souls

Unabashed

Unapologetic

And so, we lay

Heavy breathing

Together

In a rhythmic trance

We lay

Transfixed

Body to body

Soul to soul

Amoretti on its way.

Someone

Kriti Garg Agrawal

If someone is out there
Who can just listen
There are a lot of voices
That are getting louder by the day

My head is going to explode
It seems

As if my tongue
Could've been more useful
For a mute

No use of it whatsoever
if people around me
Can't even pay heed
To the words coming out of it

If someone's out there
Holler at me
Coz my ears have been trained well
Even if my throat
Has been choked forever

I Grew Up

Kriti Garg Agrawal

I grew up today when I finally realised, when I faced the nightmare with my open eyes, when i shivered for someone to hold me and had to hug myself, when the world seemed to come to an end but had to tie a knot of hope.

I grew up today when I became the victim, when I woke up with a jolt, when I paced up and down alone trying to figure out, when I scratched and scratched but did not come up with a solution.

I grew up today when I realised mom is not here to rescue me from the hell I was falling in, when no-one but I understood that there is not just one problem but many, when I went and became a pawn instead of daddy's little princess.

I grew up today when I finally understood that being good will only bring you harm, when only I was there to hold my hand and show the path towards the light, when I console myself towards not saying "goodbye!" yet.

I grew up today when I ignored him and did not listen to any threats, when I went home and prepared food waiting for the someone whom I love with all my heart, when I confronted myself and found out I was nothing but a stupid little girl.

But as I know today that little girl is buried deep inside with all her toys, hopes and dreams. And all that is left is this grown up who does not need anyone to find her shoe, to rescue her from the dragon, to wake her from the sleeping curse.

As she now hymns her own tune, and that tune contains all the verses that show how she became the piece that fits just right in this big jigsaw puzzle they call "Life."

Insanity Land

Kriti Garg Agrawal

I have witnessed many characters
I have talked to many
I have read their faces
Read their minds
And understood their souls

But it happens very rarely
That some of those
Leave a piece of them behind
For you to cherish and hold
For an eternity, probably longer

These are the ones
Who are probably more hurt
More cheerful
More experienced
And even more cruel
Than most of us

The pieces left behind
Can change the life
The point of view
The sense of knowing things
And the reader itself

Me… Oh yes!
I've read a lot of pages
Pages that make a book
Pages that make autobiographies
Pages that make a course
Pages that make a novel

Somehow all of those
All the pages, novels combined
Have changed the way act
Have blurred the lines

To identify the difference
The exact contrast
Of what is black
And what is white
They left me in the grey area

The grey area….
Hard to explain really
Nothing makes much sense
Conflict at every point
Awesome and confusing both

Choosing between sanity
And what they call insanity
Both playing tug-of-war
With the little brain of mine
Uh! So exhausting

I still remember
That remarkable moment
That precise hour
The exact minute
And even the second

I crossed that arbitrary line
And ended up in
The Insanity Land
Just so overwhelming
Most beautiful place ever

I really want to tell you
How i felt being there
Not pretending
So many characters showing up
At very odd moments

But it's just difficult
The tale can't be told
It's the one
To be experienced
To be lived

To be…..
Oh! Cookie….

Co-authors
in this anthology

Abhishek Agarwal

Abhishek (being_me_av) is an XLRI Jamshedpur alumni, a serial entrepreneur from Bangalore and an internationally authenticated and certified business, career, life, and success coach. He has a deep passion for writing. He writes real content on various topics and is a thought leader, visionary and polymath who shares a deep love for food, nutrition, running and travelling. His motto is, 'Don't live a life; live a lifestyle.'

Neeraja Krishnaswami

Neeraja Krishnaswami is a postgraduate in Business Management, an Accounts Executive with her father, and a blogger by choice. Writing being her passion, she has participated in Poetry and Story writing competitions and is a co-author in anthologies. Apart from writing, her hobbies are singing, painting and landscape photography. She can be contacted through her IG handles @neerajak_94 and @nkaysfictionalparadise.

Vaishnavi Tawade

Vaishnavi Tawade is an aspiring Counselling Psychologist based in Mumbai, India. Apart from her interest in Psychology, Vaishnavi is also extremely passionate about writing. She enjoys new experiences and believes that the world can be

a better place if people show love, kindness, and empathy towards each other.

Maxine Mathew

Maxine Mathew is an ardent bibliophile, a Shakespeare buff, and a voracious watcher of sitcoms with strong women characters. During her time away from her corporate job, one would find her snuggled away under a

blanket, devouring a book, or catching up on the latest season of my favourite sitcoms, preferably with a nice cup of strong tea.

Ginni Malik

Ginni Malik is a professional healer who has been guiding people to transform their lives for the past nine years. She has expertise in theta healing and access consciousness as well as angel card reading and coffee cup reading.

Bornali Nath Dowerah

Bornali Nath Dowerah (M.A., NET, M.Phil.) is an Assistant Professor of English, Manohari Devi Kanoi Girls' College, Dibrugarh, Assam, India. She has submitted her PhD to Dibrugarh University, Assam. She has authored six books—Literature Reader, Critical Perspectives, Kobitaar Xoraai, Crossroads, Rāmdhenu and Tiny Tales. She specialises in ELT, EAP, queer young adult literature, fiction studies and psychoanalysis.

Hiya Banerjee

Hiya is a high school student who enjoys communicating with people and getting to know them. Besides expressing herself creatively through writing about sensitive topics, she loves to weave her experiences and thoughts and pen them down.

Kriti Garg Agrawal

Kriti is a budding writer with an active imagination and an equally calm façade. She might not utter a thousand words, but her works speak volumes. Kriti is a free spirit and believes in relying on her own wings to carry her to the top.

Aksheeta Chandok (Ash)

Referred to as '*chalta phirta* Bollywood', Aksheeta is a nineteen-year-old Delhi-ite pursuing he   r Bachelor's in Economics and Marketing Management, BHU Varanasi. She finds solace in aesthetics, and you can find her clicking pictures of everything she comes across.

Anurag Pandey

Anurag Pandey, 25-year-old from the streets of Kanpur. Passionate about machines, did graduation in Mech Engg. from Chennai & working as Senior R&D Engineer at Hyundai MOBIS, Hyderabad. Apart from machines he likes to spend his time getting lost in the world of content writing. His narratives are mostly related to love, life, and struggles of the common man.

Hrishikesh Mokashi

Hrishikesh Mokashi is a B Com student at Savitribai Phule Pune University, Maharashtra. An avid reader, poet and a blogger, he generally loves to read mystery stories and autobiographies of famous personalities. A fitness  enthusiast, he is also a blogger who loves to write fictions.

INKFEATHERS PUBLISHING

India's Most Author Friendly Publishing House

Stay updated about the latest books, anthologies, events, exclusive offers, contests, product giveaways and other things that we do to support authors.

 Inkfeathers Publishing

 @InkfeathersPublishing

 @_Inkfeathers

 @Inkfeathers

 Inkfeathers.com

We'd love to connect with you!